CREATIVE COMPANIES

THE STORY OF McDONALD'S

SARA GILBERT

JAICO PUBLISHING HOUSE

Ahmedabad Bangalore Chennai
Delhi Hyderabad Kolkata Mumbai

Published by Jaico Publishing House
A-2 Jash Chambers, 7-A Sir Phirozshah Mehta Road
Fort, Mumbai - 400 001
jaicopub@jaicobooks.com
www.jaicobooks.com

Published in arrangement with
The Creative Company
123 South Broad Street, Mankato, MN 56001, USA

To be sold only in India, Bangladesh, Bhutan,
Pakistan, Nepal, Sri Lanka and the Maldives.

Design and Production by Zeno Design

Photographs by Alamy (Ferruccio, Kevin Foy, Jeff Greenberg, Kim Karpeles, Oleksiy Maksmenko, Jiri Rezac, Helene Rogers, Stephen Saks Photography, Vario Images GmbH & Co.KG, Jim West), Corbis (Louie Psihoyos), Getty Images (Tim Boyle, Focus on Sport, LUI JIN/AFP, Guang Niu, Thos Robinson, Art Shay//Time Life Pictures, Brendan Smialowski, Mario Tama)

THE STORY OF McDONALD'S
ISBN 978-81-8495-771-6

First Jaico Impression: 2015
Sixth Jaico Impression: 2019

Page design and layout: Special Effects, Mumbai

Printed by
Trinity Academy For Corporate Training Limited, Mumbai

CREATIVE COMPANIES

THE STORY OF McDONALD'S

McDonald's

On April 15, 1955, the first McDonald's restaurant opened in Des Plaines, Illinois, with cheeseburgers, French fries, and milk shakes on the menu with cheerful men and women serving up the food from behind a counter. Five decades later, on April 15, 2005, a new restaurant opened just a few miles away—a 24,000-square-foot (2,230 sq. m) McDonald's built in downtown Chicago to commemorate the iconic restaurant's 50th anniversary. The new McDonald's was outfitted with 60-foot (18 m) Golden Arches, double drive-thru lanes, and seating for 300—a far cry from the original drive-in with no indoor seating. But despite the physical differences and a host of new menu options, the commitment to quality and customer service that had started half a century earlier was the same as ever.

1
Beginning with Burgers

It was milk shakes, not hamburgers, which originally lured Ray Kroc to San Bernardino, California, in 1954. Restaurateurs Dick and Mac McDonald were operating eight multi-mixer machines, which were used to make milk shakes, in their drive-in, and Kroc, who sold the machines, was eager to learn why. So he flew from his home in Chicago to California to see the McDonald's restaurant for himself.

Kroc was surprised to see a line of cars and people form outside the service window at lunch. When he asked one of the men in line what the attraction was, the customer said, "You'll get the best hamburger you ever ate for 15 cents." Kroc polled the other people waiting and learned that many of them came for a lunch of burgers, fries, and milk shakes every day. He was so impressed that, the next day, in a meeting with the McDonald brothers, he suggested that they franchise their Speedee Service System, which allowed them to make their limited menu quickly using an efficient kitchen setup, in restaurants across the country.

The brothers, who had already licensed the concept to a handful of other restaurants in the West, were leery of attempting to franchise their fast-food restaurant on a large scale. They didn't want the burden of regulating the restaurants, but Kroc volunteered to handle that for them.

With the hesitant blessing of the McDonald brothers, Kroc formed a franchising company, originally known as McDonald's System, Inc., on March 2, 1955, in Oak Brook, Illinois. His original intent was to establish franchisees of the McDonald's restaurant to drive sales of the multi-mixer machines he sold. And although his sole source of income until 1961 would be the $12,000 salary he earned from selling multi-mixers (he had decided not to take a salary from McDonald's until the business had turned a profit), it quickly became clear that 15-cent burgers, not milk shakes, would be the base of his business.

Kroc opened his first McDonald's in Des Plaines, Illinois, in April 1955, often helping sweep floors and clean restrooms himself to get the business off the ground, and to establish what would become the operating principle for the company: "Quality, Service, Cleanliness, and Value." Fred Turner, who would later become president and eventually chairman of the company, was one of the first grill men at the restaurant. He later recalled seeing his boss walk around, picking up every bit of McDonald's litter

McDonald's original Speedee Service System logo promised inexpensive hamburgers served quickly he found. "He'd come into the store with both hands full of cups and wrappers," Turner said. "He was the store's outside pickup man."

Kroc was also busy finding franchisees to open more McDonald's. In his first year, the company built 18 restaurants, almost half of them in California. When it became clear that trying to maintain uniform standards at restaurants 2,000 miles (3,218 km) away was nearly impossible, Kroc decided to focus his efforts closer to Chicago. His first real taste of success came in Waukegan, Illinois, where a franchise opened on May 26, 1955. On its first day, the store almost ran out of buns before 5:00 P.M. and sold $450 worth of food; the following day, sales nearly doubled, and lines stretched

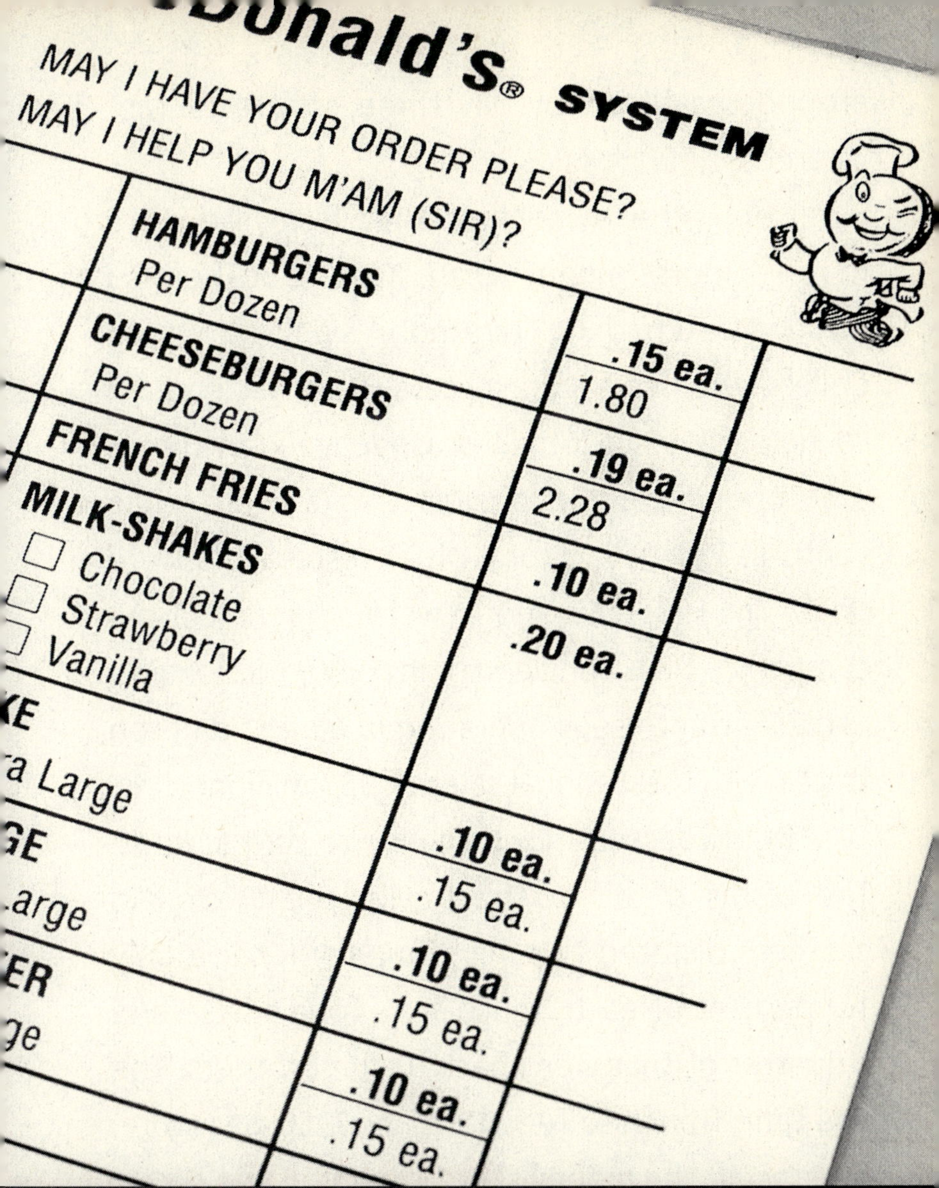

...Donald's® SYSTEM

MAY I HAVE YOUR ORDER PLEASE?
MAY I HELP YOU M'AM (SIR)?

HAMBURGERS Per Dozen	**.15 ea.** 1.80	
CHEESEBURGERS Per Dozen	**.19 ea.** 2.28	
FRENCH FRIES	**.10 ea.**	
MILK-SHAKES ☐ Chocolate ☐ Strawberry ☐ Vanilla	**.20 ea.**	
KE a Large	**.10 ea.** .15 ea.	
GE Large	**.10 ea.** .15 ea.	
ER ge	**.10 ea.** .15 ea.	

McDonald's found success in the 1950s using a basic menu and ordering system built around burgers and shakes around the block. By day three, the restaurant cleared $1,000 in sales.

Soon, the owners of that franchise were making more money than Kroc. But he had achieved something far more significant than dollars—he had found success. That was enough to help convince other prospective franchisees that opening a McDonald's was a worthwhile venture. By 1958, a total of 34 restaurants were open; in 1959, 67 more were added. By the company's fifth anniversary in 1960, McDonald's had 200 franchisees operating in almost a dozen states with total annual sales of $37 million.

But Kroc was still struggling to turn a profit. The terms of his contract with the McDonald brothers dictated that his company receive only 1.9 percent of each franchisee's food sales—and a quarter of that went back to the brothers. The one-time franchise fee was only $950 per store. As a result, the money Kroc brought in was barely enough to cover the expense of helping the individual store operators get started and to pay

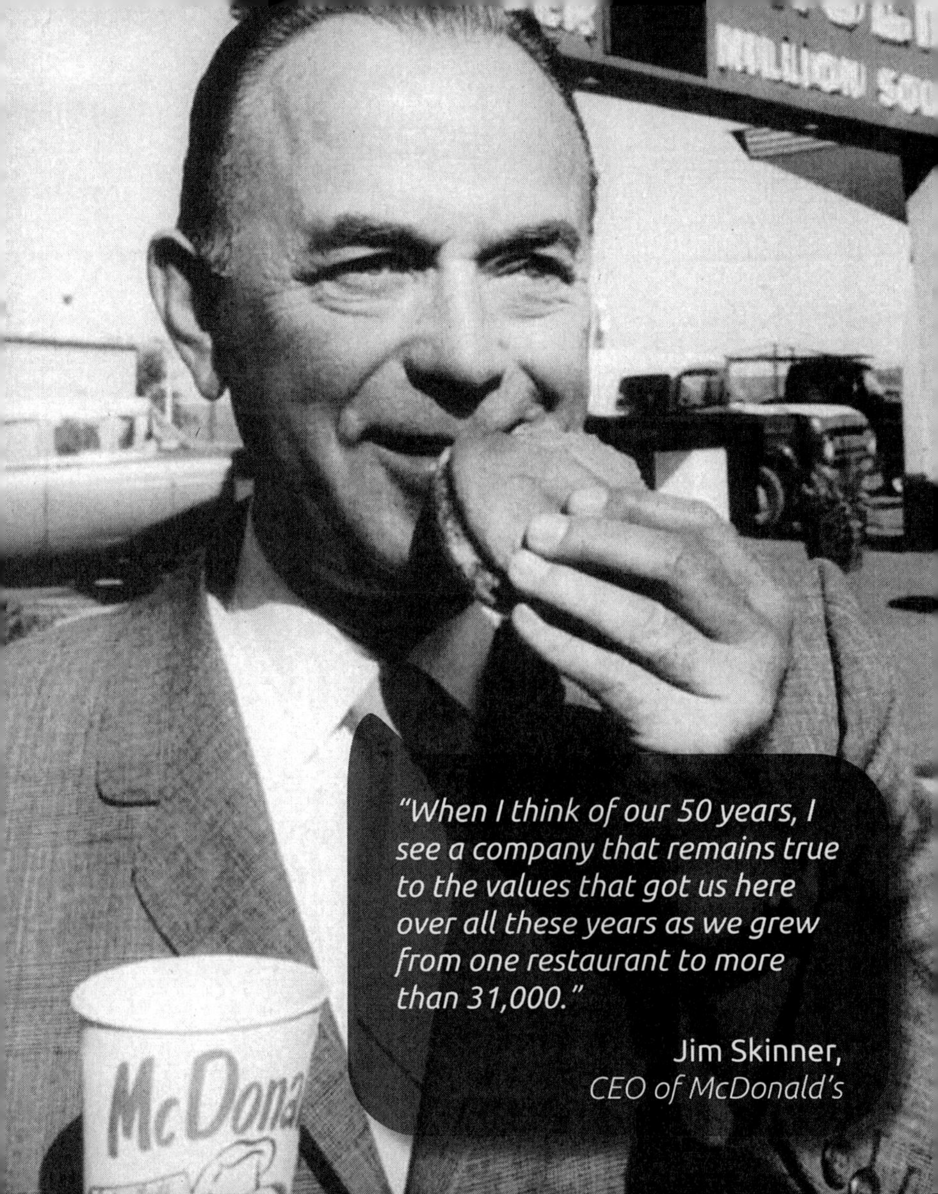

"When I think of our 50 years, I see a company that remains true to the values that got us here over all these years as we grew from one restaurant to more than 31,000."

Jim Skinner,
CEO of McDonald's

McDonald's sold nearly 50 billion hamburgers during the 29 years that Ray Kroc ran the company

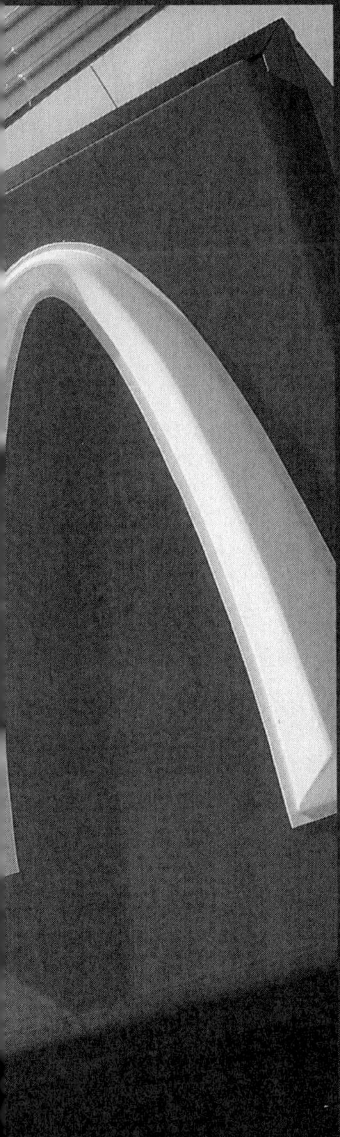

The Original Arches

When architect Stanley Meston agreed to design a building for the McDonald brothers' new restaurant in 1952, he had no idea that it would become an icon of American pop culture. He also had no idea that the very element he refused to incorporate would become its most recognizable feature. But when Dick McDonald presented him with sketches that incorporated two towering arches on either side of the building, Meston flat-out refused to add them, saying that if the arches stayed, then he left. To appease Meston, McDonald told him to leave them out. But after Meston finished his drawings, McDonald took them to a sign maker and asked him to add the arches to the plans. That sign maker added decorative, bright yellow arches that could be seen for blocks and were the most prominent part of the building. "The arches were the whole thing," McDonald said. "Without them, it was just another rectangular building."

the salaries of the growing executive team.

It was the ingenuity of one of those executives, Harry Sonneborn, that turned the tide for McDonald's. In 1957, he set up Franchise Realty Corporation to locate and lease sites for stores, then sublease the properties to the franchisees with a markup, based on a formula related to the volume of sales. The plan provided an immediate revenue stream for the company and gave Kroc more control over the franchisees and where they could be located.

The company had to go into debt to fund the rapid growth that would allow it to start profiting from its real-estate program. The best way to maximize the business's money, Kroc believed, was to purchase the rights to the McDonald's trade name and fast-food system outright from Mac and Dick McDonald, which would eliminate the percentage of sales going directly to them. The brothers asked for $2.7 million, which was much more than Kroc had available. But he and Sonneborn found lenders, obtained the necessary funds, and, in 1961, bought the brothers out. In the long run, Kroc believed, he would get a better deal.

2

McDonald's on the Map

Buying out the McDonald brothers was the start of a new era for Ray Kroc and his company. Now he was free to implement his own ideas and to control the growing network of fast-food franchises as he saw fit. He was a stickler for uniformity among all of his restaurants and insisted on a commitment to quality, cleanliness, and superb customer service from each one.

That quality control became even more important as the franchise started expanding exponentially in the 1960s, adding more than 500 locations over the course of the decade.

Marketing the restaurants became just as important. In its early days, McDonald's had invested almost nothing in national advertising, although it encouraged its franchisees to advertise locally. Its first national ad was a one-page advertisement in *Reader's Digest* in 1963, the same year that the company produced its first two television spots. In 1964, McDonald's would retain a national ad agency. By 1967, it would also establish its own internal marketing department. Soon its inventive jingles, including the memorable "You deserve a break today" slogan, and its jovial mascot, a clown named Ronald McDonald, would be all over television and radio airwaves.

But McDonald's emerging dominance was based on far more than catchy slogans and colorful clowns. In 1963, McDonald's celebrated two milestones—opening its 500th restaurant and selling its one billionth hamburger. Sales were climbing, and Kroc was taking home a handsome annual salary of about $115,000. But to really maximize the company's potential, he and the other principal owners of the company—Sonneborn, who had been named chief executive officer (CEO) in 1960, and June Martino, Kroc's long time secretary—knew they would have to take McDonald's public to raise the capital needed to help the company grow.

On April 15, 1965—a decade after Kroc's first restaurant opened—McDonald's became a publicly owned company with an initial public offering (IPO) of stock to investors at $22.50 a share. Although brokers on New York City's Wall Street, where much of the nation's stocks are traded, were wary of a business many of them had not heard of (McDonald's had not yet broken into the New York market), investors across the country were intrigued by this opportunity. By the end of the first day of trading, the price for a share had shot up to $30; within a week, it had

This museum exhibit captures the romanticism of the 1960s, a decade of rapid growth for McDonald's climbed to $36. Suddenly, McDonald's owners were millionaires.

That financial boost from the stock offering loosened the purse strings at McDonald's Corporation, as the company had been renamed. Sonneborn paid $75,000 for a three-and-a-half minute television spot during the 1965 Macy's Thanksgiving Day Parade and even agreed to sponsor a high school marching band that wore McDonald's Golden Arches on its uniforms. The investment paid off: In the month following the parade, sales increased nationwide by eight percent.

The payoff from the parade advertising led to another landmark decision. In 1966, McDonald's was approached by the CBS television network about advertising during a new sporting event: the first Super Bowl. Sonneborn bargained the $200,000 asking price down to $170,000 and purchased a similar spot on NBC, which was also televising the game, for $75,000.

It was a bit of a gamble, since it was a first-

"McDonald's and the city of Chicago have really grown together. On behalf of Chicago, thanks to McDonald's for 50 great years of service to customers, not only in Chicago but around the globe."

Richard M. Daley,
Mayor Of Chicago

From commercials to giant balloons, McDonald's has long played a part in the Macy's Thanksgiving Day Parade time broadcast of a brand-new event, but it turned out to be one of the best advertising buys McDonald's ever made. A full 41 percent of households in the United States tuned in to watch football's Green Bay Packers defeat the Kansas City Chiefs 35–10, making it the highest-rated program of the year and one of the most widely watched in television history. And McDonald's, which was the only sponsor on both networks, saw an immediate boost in sales. The chain's average sales per store for January 1967 jumped 22 percent over the same month's sales the previous year.

McDonald's was also making more money because it was expanding its menu—often due to the innovative ideas of

climbed to $36. Suddenly, McDonald's owners were millionaires.

That financial boost from the stock offering loosened the purse strings at McDonald's Corporation, as the company had been renamed. Sonneborn paid $75,000 for a three-and-a-half minute television spot during the 1965 Macy's Thanksgiving Day Parade and even agreed to sponsor a high school marching band that wore McDonald's Golden Arches on its uniforms. The investment paid off: In the month following the parade, sales increased nationwide by eight percent.

The payoff from the parade advertising led to another landmark decision. In 1966, McDonald's was approached by the CBS television network about advertising during a new sporting event: the first Super Bowl. Sonneborn bargained the $200,000 asking price down to $170,000 and purchased a similar spot on NBC, which was also televising the game, for $75,000.

It was a bit of a gamble, since it was a first-

"McDonald's and the city of Chicago have really grown together. On behalf of Chicago, thanks to McDonald's for 50 great years of service to customers, not only in Chicago but around the globe."

Richard M. Daley,
Mayor Of Chicago

From commercials to giant balloons, McDonald's has long played a part in the Macy's Thanksgiving Day Parade

The first Super Bowl was a huge success for McDonald's, as it introduced the company to millions of viewers

The Birth of the Big Mac

McDonald's most famous sandwich was born in Pittsburgh, Pennsylvania, in 1967. Jim Delligatti, who operated a dozen McDonald's restaurants in the city, wanted something bigger and better on his menu. So he started stacking burgers and buns together. He called his burger—two beef patties separated by a center section of bun and accompanied by lettuce, pickles, onion, and a "secret sauce"—the Big Mac. When he put it on his menu as a test, it cost a whopping 45 cents—quite a jump from the standard 15-cent burgers. But hungry customers were willing to pay for the Big Mac. Within months, it was being tested in more markets, and by 1968, it was available at every McDonald's restaurant in the nation. "This wasn't like discovering the light bulb," Delligatti said. "The bulb was already there. All I did was screw it in the socket."

the franchisees themselves. The Filet-O-Fish burger was introduced in 1964, the Big Mac in 1968, and the Shamrock Shake in the early 1970s. Kroc even tried a little product development on his own. Shortly before the Filet-O-Fish became a successful non-meat alternative, he tried the Hulaburger—a slice of pineapple, topped with a slice of cheese, served on a bun. It flopped.

Kroc may have struggled with new product innovation, but he didn't with new restaurants. In 1968, McDonald's Corporation opened its 1,000th location; in 1970, as it sold its five billionth hamburger, McDonald's officially reached all 50 states. But in the midst of the explosive growth, trouble sprouted. Kroc and his long time right-hand man, Harry Sonneborn, had developed differing views about how quickly the company should grow. The showdown between the two men culminated in 1967, when Sonneborn resigned at Kroc's request. When the stunned board of directors found out, they demanded to know who would be replacing him. Kroc immediately thought of Fred Turner, who at the time was the head of operations for the company. "We'll put Fred Turner in there," Kroc replied. "He's a smart guy, and he can learn. He can do it."

3
Franchise Fever

Fred Turner officially took over as president in 1968, just as the fast-food industry was exploding. Burger King, McDonald's closest competitor, was putting up 100 stores each year, and Burger Chef was just 100 locations shy of McDonald's total at the time. New regional chains were being introduced, from Jack in the Box in the West to Minnie Pearl's Chicken in the South.

Dave Thomas had also just launched Wendy's with the intention of cutting into McDonald's market share. McDonald's reign as the market leader was facing its first serious threat.

Turner decided to abandon Sonneborn's earlier plan of slowing down the addition of new stores. In fact, he went in the opposite direction entirely. "There was pent-up consumer demand throughout the system," Turner later said. "All of our markets needed more outlets." So he doubled staff in both the real estate and construction departments and embarked on an aggressive growth plan. In 1969, 211 new locations opened—a number that continued increasing until 1974, when 515 more locations were opened. By then, McDonald's had a total of 3,000 restaurants across the country and was the fast-food industry leader.

McDonald's growth was fed in part by a new trend in the American lifestyle. As the 1970s progressed, suburban housing developments were becoming popular. People were spending more time in their cars and wanted faster dining options.

But while the other fast-food franchises were being swallowed up by corporate conglomerates, McDonald's had stayed true to its core business principles. As the fast-food landscape changed, the commitment to quality and customer service that had been a part of the business from the beginning proved to be its greatest strength.

McDonald's annual sales surged past $1 billion for the first time in 1972. The opening of the first drive-thru window at a restaurant in Sierra Vista, Arizona, in 1975 helped push that figure beyond $3 billion in 1976. By then, McDonald's had a total of 4,177 stores in 22 countries.

McDonald's first foray into international franchising had come in 1967, with a restaurant in British Columbia, Canada, and another in Puerto Rico. The international market became a major source of growth in the 1970s, as the possibility for expansion within the American market began to diminish. Although Kroc had floated a number of ideas in the 1960s and '70s for diversifying the business, from a Disney-like theme park in

Burger King arose as a serious McDonald's rival in the 1960s and remains its chief competitor today

California to a German-themed restaurant in Chicago, none of them seemed like good investments of the company's cash. Instead, McDonald's focused on spreading beyond America's borders.

At the time, few other American food businesses had expanded farther than Canada. But McDonald's sought to establish franchises in Europe and Asia, where fast-food in general, and hamburgers in particular, were still unknown. The challenge was to transfer what had worked in America to new cultures. "For the old-timers, one of the really stimulating things about going international was that it meant pioneering again," Turner later said.

But there was still pioneering to be done at home as well. As

McDonald's found eager patrons in countries such as China, where traditional architecture embraced the golden arches

McDonald's place in society grew, its menu had to grow with it. The launch of a breakfast line, for example, began with the Egg McMuffin—an idea that started at a restaurant in California and was introduced throughout the McDonald's system in 1973. The burger was made with eggs fried on the grill in Teflon-coated rings the size of an English muffin, then topped with grilled Canadian bacon.

In 1979, the company started selling Happy Meals as an occasional promotional product. Although the idea was more about the packaging than a new product, it had an immediate impact on the sales. Originally, hamburgers, French fries, and a soft drink were served in collectible boxes designed as circus train cars; children could collect the

"All growth will end, and McDonald's has cheated that law time and time again. They are one of the few companies that has taken its original innovation and continued to find new ways to do things differently."

James Schrager,
University of Chicago Professor

McDonald's Happy Meals packaging and toys often tie in with popular kids' movies of the time

McDonald's
RAY A. KRO
IN 1955 RAY A. KROC ESTABL
MCDONALD'S SYSTEM WITH THE HIGHEST STAN
QUALITY, SERVICE, CLEANLINESS, AND VALUE.
PERSISTENCE, AND LEADERSHIP HAVE GUIDED MC
NE LOCATION IN DES PLAINES, ILLINOIS TO THE

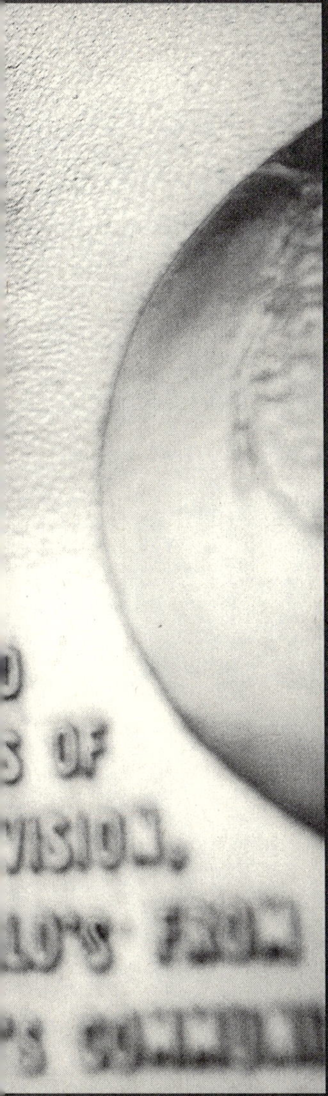

The Kroc Files

More than half of Ray Kroc's life was over by the time he discovered McDonald's in 1954. He'd already been trained as a World War I ambulance driver for the Red Cross (working with cartoon pioneer Walt Disney), a piano player, a paper cup salesman, and a dancer by the time his job of selling multi-mixer milk shake machines took him to the McDonald's drive-in in San Bernardino, California, in 1954. But spreading the McDonald's concept across the country became his life's work. "I was 52 years old," he said. "I had diabetes and incipient arthritis. I had lost my gall bladder and most of my thyroid gland in earlier campaigns, but I was convinced that the best was ahead of me." Kroc, who was born in Oak Park, Illinois, in 1902 and died in 1984, devoted the final 30 years of his life to building McDonald's into the largest fast-food company in the world.

whole set during a designated time frame. Happy Meals (which now usually include a small toy or prize) soon became so popular that they earned a spot on the menu year-round.

The development of one of McDonald's most popular menu items—chicken nuggets—came in response to changing American tastes. As the 1980s began, people were choosing to eat less beef, and Kroc wanted to introduce a chicken entrée. He even hired a chef, Rene Arend, to help. But Arend's early efforts—a deep fried chicken potpie, for example—weren't working either. It was when Arend took a break from chicken and started experimenting with "Onion Nuggets"—bite-sized chunks of battered onions—that Turner, by then the CEO, took note. "Why not try chicken nuggets instead?" he suggested.

By 1983, the nuggets were ready to roll out; by 1985, McNuggets accounted for more than $700 million of McDonald's approximately $11 billion in sales, and McDonald's had become the second-largest chicken retailer in the fast-food industry, just behind Kentucky Fried Chicken. But Ray Kroc, long known as the hamburger king, wasn't around to compare sales figures with Colonel Sanders, the chicken king. Late in 1983, McDonald's founder suffered a series of strokes and was hospitalized. Although he had worked full-time until then, he never returned to his office again. In January 1984, at the age of 82, Ray Kroc died.

4

Changing of the McGuard

McDonald's celebrated its 30th birthday in 1985 having surpassed Ray Kroc's wildest dreams for the company. Sales had exceeded $10 billion. More than 50 billion hamburgers had been sold at approximately 8,300 restaurants in 36 countries.

And the company was still in growth mode: on average, a new McDonald's restaurant opened somewhere in the world every 17 hours. By 1988, there would be more than 10,000 McDonald's in operation.

Much of that development flourished under new leadership. Michael Quinlan, who had started working with the company in 1963 as a part-time mail clerk, took over as president in 1982 and succeeded Turner as CEO in 1987. In his first year as CEO, Quinlan opened 600 new restaurants around the world, laying the groundwork for unprecedented expansion by the company. Quinlan was so aggressive that, at one point in the 1980s, McDonald's was opening five stores a day, adamantly defying the notion that the fast-food market was saturated, or filled to capacity. "Saturation applies to our competitors, not to us," Quinlan confidently told shareholders in 1989.

Within a decade, Quinlan's efforts had introduced McDonald's to a total of 106 countries and had more than doubled company sales.

When the first McDonald's opened in Moscow, Russia, in 1990, more than 30,000 people waited in the cold to visit the restaurant; two years later, an opening in Beijing, China, attracted 40,000 customers on the first day. Lines at restaurants in Poland and Israel made news as well. With a network of more than 22,000 restaurants worldwide, McDonald's had, by 1997, displaced Coca-Cola as the world's best-known brand, according to Interbrand, a London-based consulting firm.

But amid such international acclaim, the brand was becoming beleaguered back home. For one thing, franchisees were growing concerned that the rapid rate of growth, which often placed new restaurants within blocks of existing locations, would cut into their sales. With fast-food restaurants now quite common in the U.S., domestic sales were leveling off by the mid-1990s.

On top of that, the public perception of the restaurants was shifting. As more people became aware of the importance of healthy food choices,

As America filled with McDonald's restaurants in the late '80s, the company looked at markets abroad consumers were increasingly concerned that the food served at McDonald's, including the deep-fried items and those made from animal products, was laden with fat, salt, and cholesterol. More consumers also became worried about the impact that McDonald's packaging products—many of which were made of foam—had on the environment.

The company's efforts to address those problems were only partially successful. Although salads had been added to the menu in 1987, further attempts to diversify the chain's fare didn't go as well. McDonald's tried fried chicken, pasta, fajitas, and pizza, but none caught on with customers. Even the McLean Deluxe, a 91 percent fat-free beef patty that was introduced

Some environmentalist groups have criticized McDonald's paper and packaging consumption as wasteful in 1991 as a response to health concerns, fizzled, remaining on the menu for only five years before disappearing.

Although tinkering with the menu didn't solve McDonald's health problem, the company's efforts to soften its impact on the environment were more successful. In 1990, the company made a commitment to spend at least $100 million annually on recycled products, from chairs and table tops to toilet tissue and corrugated cartons. The company worked with the U.S. Environmental Defense Fund to develop a comprehensive solid waste reduction program; switching to paper wraps for burgers, which had previously been served in plastic containers, resulted in a 90 percent reduction in waste from wrapping materials. "McDonald's is proving that a company can do well by doing good," said Fred Krupp, the executive director of the Environmental Defense Fund.

Yet even in the midst of such improvements, consumers were drifting away from McDonald's

> *"If I were going to live to be a hundred, I'd be down here [in the offices] every day of the week."*
>
> Ray Kroc

Although McDonald's has tried many menu items, hamburgers remain the heart of its business

McDonald's Weight Problem

In the summer of 2002, two overweight teenagers from New York City filed a class-action lawsuit against McDonald's. The girls, both of whom ate at the restaurant frequently, claimed that the Big Macs, Egg McMuffins, and Happy Meals that they consumed had made them obese and unhealthy. They contended that McDonald's had not adequately disclosed the amount of fat, sugar, salt, and cholesterol in its food. A judge twice dismissed the case, saying that McDonald's could not be blamed by consumers who chose to eat its food, and that its advertising was not deceptive. "We trusted that common sense would prevail in the case, and it did," McDonald's spokesperson Lisa Howard said. "McDonald's food can fit into a healthy, well-balanced diet based upon the choice and variety available on our menu." The lawsuit was revived in appeals court in January 2005; no decision had been reached by early 2008.

and toward competitors such as Wendy's and Burger King, which had launched the Big King burger to compete with the Big Mac. It soon became apparent to McDonald's management team that the company could not sustain such an explosive growth, at least not within the U.S. After opening 1,130 stores domestically in 1995, it scaled back to 400 additions in 1997. In addition, plans to open hundreds of smaller units in Wal-Mart stores and gas stations were shelved because the test sites weren't meeting their goals.

In the wake of taste tests that showed that consumers preferred the taste of burgers from other restaurants, McDonald's also decided to go back to the kitchen to rethink some of its food production. The resulting Arch Deluxe, a quarter-pound burger served with bacon, lettuce, tomato, and a "secret" mustard sauce, was introduced in 1996. Although McDonald's marketed the burger and its companion burgers—the Fish Filet Deluxe, Grilled Chicken Deluxe, and Crispy

Chicken Deluxe—as "grown-up" options, the new line failed miserably. They were priced too high (between $2.25 and $3.00) and had too many calories, consumers said. And the marketing campaign, which featured kids and even the gregarious Ronald McDonald grimacing with distaste, turned many people off.

In the middle of 1998, Quinlan resigned as CEO and was replaced by Jack Greenberg, the head of American operations for McDonald's. Quinlan, who stayed on as chairman of the company, said that it was time for a change. "I think it's time to utilize the tremendous depth of management skills at McDonald's as we move into the next century," he said.

5
Trying for a Turnaround

Greenberg joined a relatively new crew of McDonald's executives when he took over as CEO. McDonald's had long been known for shepherding executives from its own grills to the corporate suites, but now, hearing from both Wall Street and its own franchisees that its business strategies were stale, the company decided to look for help from the outside.

A former executive from the Long John Silver's seafood company had already been tapped to overhaul menu planning, and a former leader with Pizza Hut was brought in to lead the American sales force.

A month after Greenberg was installed as CEO, he announced that, for the first time in its 43-year history, McDonald's Corporation would have to make job cuts. About 525 jobs at the corporate headquarters—almost a quarter of the staff—were slashed. That led to another first since the company had gone public in 1965—net income dropped, from $1.64 billion in 1997 to $1.5 billion in 1998.

It was apparent that McDonald's could no longer rely on burgers alone to make money. A series of acquisitions, beginning in 1998 with the purchase of a minority stake in the Colorado-based Chipotle Mexican Grill chain and culminating in the purchase of the bankrupt Boston Market family dining chain in 2000, were intended to diversify the company's holdings.

But while the company looked elsewhere for growth, its burger business was suffering. In 2002, the sales were so sluggish that the company announced another round of job cuts, as well as the closure of almost 200 restaurants, mostly in the U.S. Franchisees were frustrated by the costly new "Made for You" production system, which was introduced in 1998 to help make McDonald's foods fresher for each customer, but ended up increasing service times instead. Consumers were also rebelling against the high fat content in many items on McDonald's menu; the issue would be made even larger with the 2004 release of Super Size Me, a documentary film that showed the health problems of a man who ate nothing but McDonald's food for an entire month.

By the end of 2002, McDonald's network of almost 30,000 restaurants worldwide was struggling. The stock price had dropped by 60 percent in the course of three years, debt was adding up, while profits were declining. By late December 2002, the board of directors asked

Jack Greenberg tried to expand McDonald's business holdings after taking over as CEO in 1998

Greenberg to leave and enticed former president Jim Cantalupo out of retirement to return as CEO.

Cantalupo created a new plan that called for a dramatic decrease in new locations and for the closure of more than 700 stores that were failing. He put the company's partner brands—including Chipotle and Boston Market—on the back burner and scrapped a costly $1 billion technology project that would have changed the computer systems in all the restaurants. He started thinking about how to update the brand image to attract teenagers and young adults once again. And then he asked an old friend, Fred Turner, to come back to the company and help McDonald's refocus on its food and service. Cantalupo introduced his "Plan to

Filmmaker Morgan Spurlock attacked the high fat content of McDonald's menu in his documentary Super Size Me

Win" to the company's 1.6 million employees by saying, "I offer no false promises, no silver bullets. However, under my leadership, neither failure nor second place is an option."

By the end of 2003, Cantalupo's efforts were achieving results. Sales were up, including a dramatic increase at those locations that had been open for a year or more, and customers were coming back for burgers (now generally priced around $1), thanks in part to the new "I'm Lovin' It" ad campaign, which featured everyday people from around the world singing a catchy jingle about their affection for McDonald's. As the 60-year-old CEO prepared for the annual meeting of McDonald's restaurant owners in Orlando, Florida, he was on top of the world. "Does it get any better than this?" he asked Mike Roberts, head of U.S. operations at the time. But Cantalupo wouldn't find out. The next day, he suffered a heart attack and died.

The turnaround that Cantalupo had set in motion, however, continued under his successor,

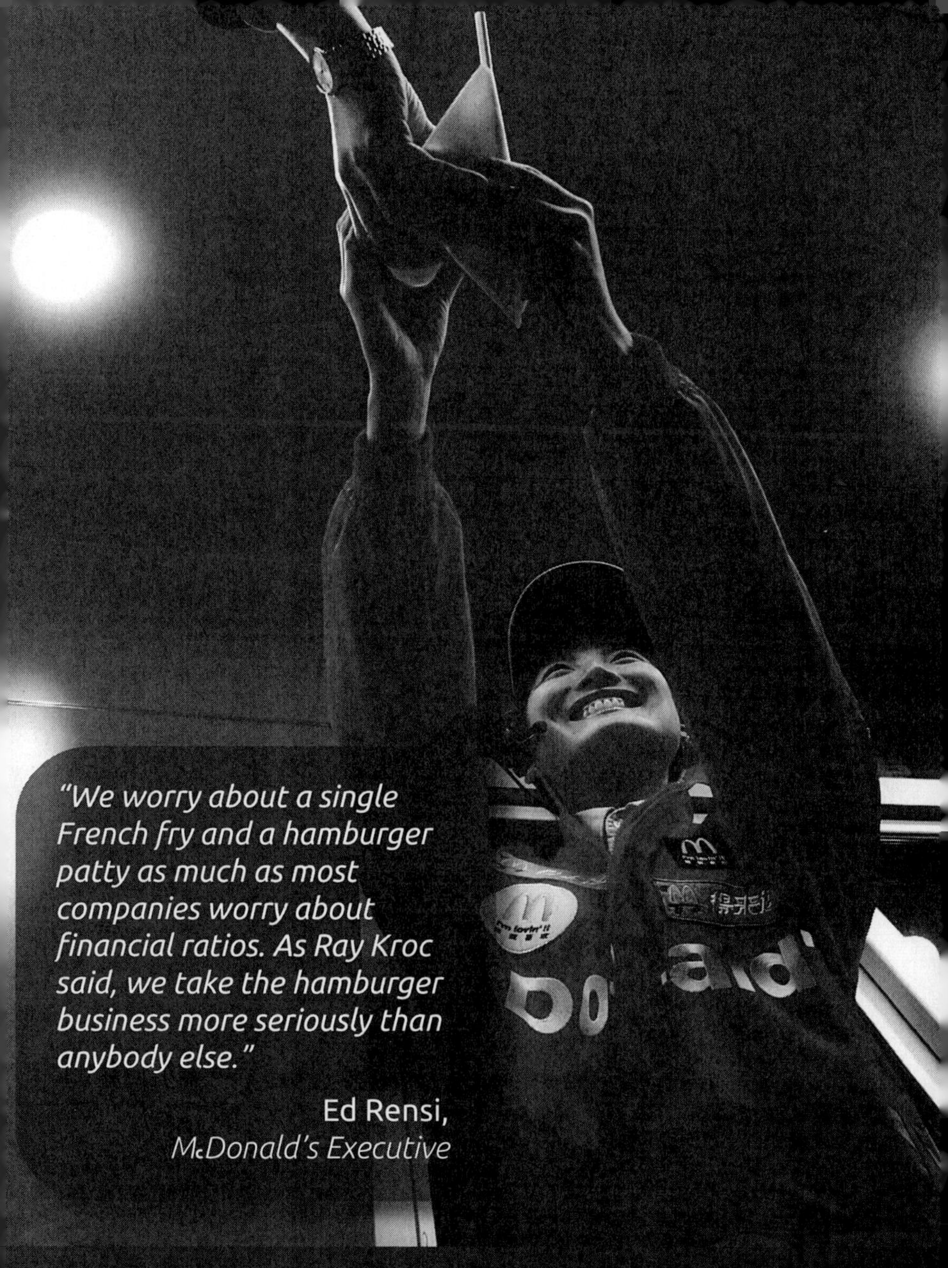

"We worry about a single French fry and a hamburger patty as much as most companies worry about financial ratios. As Ray Kroc said, we take the hamburger business more seriously than anybody else."

Ed Rensi,
McDonald's Executive

Quality customer service remains a top priority in the thousands of McDonald's restaurants today

Don

The Face of the Franchise

Almost every child in America knows Ronald McDonald. In fact, according to the 2001 book *Fast Food Nation*, only Santa Claus is more recognizable to school children than McDonald's red-haired clown. His yellow jumpsuit and floppy red shoes have been associated with the restaurant since 1963, when Willard Scott (who later became better known as the weatherman for NBC's *Today* show) first appeared with a paper cup attached to his nose and a fast-food tray propped on his head in local McDonald's commercials in Washington, D.C. By 1965, Ronald had become the cornerstone of the franchise's advertising campaigns, and Scott had been replaced by a younger, trimmer actor. Although Ronald's costume has evolved over the years, his appearance—from the red wig and nose to the ballooning yellow suit and striped socks—has become part of the corporate identity. The clown even has an official title: Chief Happiness Officer.

Jim Skinner. By the time it celebrated its 50th birthday in 2005, McDonald's was reporting an improved cash flow, higher profits, and continued growth around the world.

McDonald's fortunes continued to rise in the years that followed. By the end of 2006, as restaurants instituted longer hours and added premium products, from salads to coffee, to their menus, the price of McDonald's shares had risen by 25 percent. Although the company remained cautious of rapid expansion, it was looking to build at least a 100 restaurants a year in China through 2008 and to refurbish existing locations in the U.S. as well. Skinner also remained open to ideas for new products. In early 2008, for example, McDonald's unveiled plans to install coffee bars in its U.S. restaurants in order to compete against coffee companies such as Starbucks. "If we can find goods and services or a product or technology that we could leverage through 31,000 [locations], that would be the only thing we would consider," Skinner said.

That sounds like the same approach Ray Kroc took five decades earlier, when McDonald's was still a fledgling business getting off the ground in Des Plaines, Illinois. His commitment to quality, cleanliness, and unsurpassed customer service laid the groundwork for what has become the largest fast-food franchise in the world. And those basic tenets of business are what will carry it through the next half century as well.

Glossary

acquisitions the purchases of companies by other companies

board of directors a group of people in charge of making big decisions for a publicly owned company

brand the name of a product or manufacturer; a brand distinguishes a product from similar products made by other manufacturers

brokers individuals or firms that act as mediators between a buyer and seller, usually charging a fee for those services

cash flow the amounts of money received and spent by a company

conglomerates corporations consisting of several companies in different businesses

debt the condition of owing something to another person or entity

executive a decision-making leader of a company, such as the president or chief executive officer (CEO)

fast food inexpensive food, such as hamburgers and fried chicken, that is prepared and served quickly

franchise to extend a successful product or service to other businesses (called franchisees) that operate under the franchisor's trade name in exchange for a fee and often a portion of the profits

initial public offering the first sale of stock by a company to the public; it is generally done to raise funds for the company, which is then owned by investors rather than an individual or group of individuals

jingles catchy, often musical advertising slogans

lease a written agreement under which a property owner allows a tenant to use the property for a specified period of time and rent

lenders people or institutions, such as banks, that provide money to another person or business temporarily

market share the percentage of the total sales of a given type of product or service that are attributable to a particular company

net income the total income a company has after subtracting costs and expenses from the money it makes

marketing advertising and promoting a product in order to increase sales

revenue the money earned by a company; another word for income

sponsor a person or organization that finances a project or event carried out by another person or group, often as a means of advertising

Selected Bibliography

Boas, Max, and Steve Chain. Big Mac: The Unauthorized Biography of McDonald's. New York: E.P. Dutton and Co., 1976.

Greising, David, and Jim Kirk. "McDonald's Faces Big Challenge after Turning Its Fortunes Around." Chicago Tribune (July 12, 2004): 1.

Hume, Scott. "Jim Skinner: McDonald's Corp.'s CEO Seeks to Provide Stability and Continue Its Sales." Restaurants & Institutions 115, no. 4 (2005): 17–20.

Kroc, Ray. Grinding It Out: The Making of McDonald's. New York: St. Martin's Paperbacks, 1977.

Love, John F. McDonald's, Behind the Arches. New York: Bantam Books, 1986.

Pepin, Jacques. "Ray Kroc (The Time 100)." Time 152, no. 23 (1998): 176.

Index

JAICO PUBLISHING HOUSE

Elevate Your Life. Transform Your World.

ESTABLISHED IN 1946, Jaico Publishing House is home to world-transforming authors such as Sri Sri Paramahansa Yogananda, Osho, The Dalai Lama, Sri Sri Ravi Shankar, Sadhguru, Robin Sharma, Deepak Chopra, Jack Canfield, Eknath Easwaran, Devdutt Pattanaik, Khushwant Singh, John Maxwell, Brian Tracy and Stephen Hawking.

Our late founder Mr. Jaman Shah first established Jaico as a book distribution company. Sensing that independence was around the corner, he aptly named his company Jaico ('Jai' means victory in Hindi). In order to service the significant demand for affordable books in a developing nation, Mr. Shah initiated Jaico's own publications. Jaico was India's first publisher of paperback books in the English language.

While self-help, religion and philosophy, mind/body/spirit, and business titles form the cornerstone of our non-fiction list, we publish an exciting range of travel, current affairs, biography, and popular science books as well. Our renewed focus on popular fiction is evident in our new titles by a host of fresh young talent from India and abroad. Jaico's recently established Translations Division translates selected English content into nine regional languages.

In addition to being a publisher and distributor of its own titles, Jaico is a major national distributor of books of leading international and Indian publishers. With its headquarters in Mumbai, Jaico has branches and sales offices in Ahmedabad, Bangalore, Bhopal, Chennai, Delhi, Hyderabad, Kolkata and Lucknow.

SINCE 1946